Her name is Mylee, bright and keen,
but on Halloween she`s Halloweenie!
With wagging tail and happy cheer,
she brings the magic of the year.

By Sharon Marshall

It was Halloween night, and little Miss Mylee the dachshund wriggled into her pumpkin costume. Her tail wagged—tonight was full of treats and adventures!

As she trotted down the street,
she saw children in costumes,
giggling and carrying glowing
candy buckets.
Miss Mylee's long ears perked
up—something sparkly was
hiding in the bushes!

It was a tiny jack-o'-lantern, glowing all by itself. "Woof?" barked Mylee. the lantern winked at her and rolled away, as if inviting her to follow.

through pumpkins, leaves, and shadows, Mylee chased the lantern.
Suddenly-boo!
A friendly ghost kitty popped out! "Don't be afraid," said the ghost kitty. "I just need a friend to share Halloween with."

Miss Mylee wagged her tail and barked happily.

Together, the Halloweenie and the ghost kitty went trick-or-treating.

Everywhere they went, people smiled and gave them treats.

Miss Mylee dressed up in a Pumpkin so bright,
Glowing and cheeful on Halloween night.
"trick or treat!" the children would say,
And Miss Mylee laughed in a pumpkin-y-way.

Candles and Giggles filled up the air,
A night full of wonder, with joy
everywhere.

When the stars twinkled high and the
moonshone with gleam,

Miss Mylee`s pumpkin costume lit up
the dream.

With games, treats, and the kind
of memories that linger long after
the candy is gone.
Every year after, the children
would say the same thing:
Halloween wasn`t truly Halloween
without
trick and treat with Miss Mylee

By the end of the night, Miss Mylee had made a new friend, and Halloween was brighter than ever.

She curled up in her bed, dreaming of candy corn and glowing pumpkins.
the End.

Tick or-or Treat.

HAPPY
HALLOWEEN